THE BOY WHO MET HITLER

This book is dedicated to my family
and the village of Whitegate.

First published in 1999 by
Mercier Press
PO Box 5 5 French Church St Cork
Tel: (021) 275040; Fax (021) 274969
E.mail: books@mercier.ie
16 Hume Street Dublin 2
Tel: (01) 661 5299; Fax: (01) 661 8583
E.mail: books@marino.ie

Trade enquiries to CMD Distribution
55A Spruce Avenue
Stillorgan Industrial Park
Blackrock County Dublin
Tel: (01) 294 2556; Fax: (01) 294 2564
E.mail: cmd@columba.ie

© Bill Wall 1999

ISBN 1 85635 269 2

10 9 8 7 6 5 4 3 2 1

A CIP record for this title is available
from the British Library

Cover illustration by Caroline Hyland
Cover design by SPACE
Printed in Ireland by ColourBooks,
Baldoyle Industrial Estate, Dublin 13

THE BOY WHO MET HITLER

BILL WALL

MERCIER PRESS

FOREWORD

Mine is a storytelling family. We tell each other the past and each generation makes the past new for the next. This book comes from the stories of my family. My father and mother are in it and my uncles J. J. and Dónal Regan, who fought Hitler in World War II. Dónal was lost at sea when his ship the *Neptune* sank in a minefield with the loss of all hands and so I never knew him. But J. J. survived four years of Arctic convoys and I remember him as a wonderful, mischievous man. My aunt is in it too and many of the people I grew up with. I have used some of their pictures, old family photographs, to try to give you some idea of what they looked like, but I have played one or two tricks. One of them, for example, is a photograph of me at the same age as Mike. But this book is not all about facts and history. It is a book about a boy and a girl who grow up in wartime, and even though the war is far away, it touches their hearts and changes their lives, as wars always do.

CONTENTS

1

MR HANLEY AND MR HITLER

Jessie

Jessie and me were best friends so when the boy who met Hitler turned up, Jessie, naturally, said we shouldn't play with him. Jessie said that he was just a common sort of boy and I agreed with her because I always agreed with her in those days. She was my best friend after all. She had a way of saying things that made them sound like they were true. I suppose I was afraid to contradict her. And she lived in a big house with a toilet inside and I didn't. She *knew* what a common sort of boy was, so she said, and she didn't like them.

On the other hand, I was inclined to suspect that I was more than a bit common myself. I didn't like to draw attention to it, so I always agreed.

The trouble was, I really wanted to find out about Hitler, because that was 1940 and the Second World War was raging in Europe and everyone was talking about it. My dad was forever reading pieces out of the newspaper about him. He said that Hitler was a very dangerous man. He said he would like to take over the whole world if only he could. My mam said that he was causing a lot of trouble and there would be many a mother losing her sons before Mr Hitler decided to retire. My mam didn't like people who caused wars at all; she always said so.

So when Jessie said that about not playing with the boy who met Hitler, I agreed with her, but deep down I was planning to talk to him some time when she wasn't around. I was saving up all the questions I could think of to ask him.

Master Hanley, our teacher, was very inter-esting about the war. There was a big map of the world on the wall of our classroom and all the parts of the world that were ruled by England were coloured red, and every time we came to do history Master Hanley would point to these red bits and say, 'This is the British Empire, boys and girls. But by the time Mr Hitler is finished with it, all these places will be a different colour altogether.' He thought that Hitler was going to conquer the whole world. He said that Hitler couldn't be beaten, that he had the best tanks and the best planes and the best submarines in the whole world.

Master Hanley hated England. He said that England was too big for its boots and that Germany was going to take it down a size.

He would make us trace out a map of Europe and mark in all the countries. Then he would make us draw little crooked crosses all over France and Holland and Denmark and he would say that all those countries were in Germany's hands. He would show us how the big bombers flew over the English channel and dropped bombs on English cities. He called it the *blitzkrieg* and he said that word meant 'lightning war'. He said that the German army was as fast as lightning and when it struck it left nothing standing.

Jessie was always in trouble with Master Hanley over Hitler. She told me that she knew that Master Hanley was a liar. 'He doesn't know the first thing about it,' she used to say. 'My brothers know. They're in the Navy.' She would stand up in class and tell Master Hanley that he was wrong about England being beaten. 'The Navy will save England,' she would tell him. 'My brothers said so.'

Jessie's big brothers went away to sea in the British Royal Navy when I was about three or four. I don't remember them going away the first time, but they were back on a holiday once and when the time came for them to go back, I got up early to say goodbye. I heard the sound of their boots coming down the hill and I ran out. I saw them marching away. They weren't wearing uniforms but they had big boots on their feet and they marched in step the way soldiers do. I called out, 'Goodbye J. J., Goodbye Dan!' and they called back, 'Cheerio mate!'

J. J. left a job in the Post Office to join the British Navy, or so my mam always said. She couldn't understand why he left a good job behind, but I could. Who would want to work in the Post Office if he could be out on a ship instead. I knew that J. J. went away for the adventure.

'If he did,' my mam used to say, 'he got more than he bargained for with this war.'

Master Hanley always said that the German submarines would destroy the Navy. 'The sub-

J. J. and shipmate at sea

marine,' he would say, 'strikes when it is least expected. It creeps up on the enemy and fires its torpedoes before anyone knows it's there. There is no defence against the submarine.'

This made Jessie cry. I think she cried because her brothers were in the ships and the submarines weren't giving the ships a fair chance. Jessie and myself were always up for a fair chance. We didn't agree with sneaking around and ambushing fellows. And then again maybe she cried because Master Hanley always picked on her when he was explaining about the war. He would ask her questions like, 'Do you think Churchill might be killed in the bombing?' Churchill was the Prime Minister of England. Master Hanley always called him 'Churchill' but called Hitler 'Mr Hitler'. He had a terrible down on England.

'Who are you up for?' Jessie used to ask me. 'Hitler or Churchill?'

I always said I was up for Churchill, but that was because of her. I would never have said anything to hurt Jessie. My dad said that Churchill was a big fat man who always smoked a cigar. He read me some of his speeches and he certainly sounded very sure of himself. When the German aeroplanes were attacking England every day, Churchill said that England would never be defeated. He said he would fight them on the beaches and all over England. I think that frightened Hitler off because he didn't come over. He stopped at the coast of France and only sent his planes over to drop bombs on the cities in England. Jessie said that was a cowardly thing to do. She said if Hitler was any good at all he would have come across the Channel himself.

'He's a coward,' she said. 'He should come over and do his own dirty work.' She had a tiny piece of black cloth cut in the shape of a moustache that she could stick under her nose and then she would pull her hair down over one eye and walk around kicking her feet very high in the air and holding her arm out straight. She said that was the way Hitler walked. She would make up words that really sounded like they were German and she would wave her hands around and jump up and down when she said them.

'Gesessen der shmashen der unter pimple von worsten fumpenworstenhorser!' she would shout. Her brothers told her that this was the way Hitler talked. I thought it was very funny.

'My brother is on the *Hood*,' she told Master Hanley one day. 'That is the finest battleship in the world. He's a petty officer.'

'And why couldn't he join the Irish Army?' Master Hanley asked. 'Why did he go to the enemy for work?'

That was Jessie's brother Dan. He joined the Navy because he couldn't get a job. There was no work in those days and a lot of the boys around my home went away to sea. Most of them joined the British Navy because there was no Irish navy. For hundreds of years boys and men have had to leave the villages around where I live. They went away to sea. Some of them went fishing on the fleets, or on Irish trawlers. Some of them went to the Navy. Sometimes when some boy drowned, the family put his name on the headstone in Corkbeg graveyard. After his name they just wrote, 'Lost at Sea'. The church is named for Saint Erasmus, the patron saint of seafarers. Nearly every house has a connection with the sea if you go back far enough.

'England is not the enemy,' Jessie told old Master Hanley.

'It is.'

'It is not!'

'Didn't we have to fight them ourselves?' Master Hanley said. 'Didn't we have to drive them out of our country? Didn't they send the Black and Tans over to burn us out of our homes? Didn't they rob this country for centuries?' He would go on like this for a bit until tears came into his eyes and he turned away. We didn't mind him because we all knew he had a down on England.

But Jessie hated him for it. On the way home afterwards she would tell me all the things she was going to do to get her revenge. 'When the war is over I'm going to write to Mr Churchill and tell him. He'll send a spy over to poison old Hanley. Or I might kill him myself. I saw my dad putting down poison for the rats last week. I could easily get some. I could put it in old Hanley's sandwiches when he's not looking.'

'Or we could ambush him,' I might suggest. 'When he's on his way to Maclean's.' Master Hanley went down to Maclean's every night at eight o'clock and came home just before closing time. It would be easy to ambush him before he got to the pub.

'Don't be silly,' she would say. 'It has to be *clandestine*.'

'Clandestine' was one of her favourite words.

She told me once that it meant something that was bright and dangerous all at once, and something secret, like a candle that would light your way in the dark but if you dropped it it could set fire to something. That was what Jessie said clandestine meant.

When the boy who met Hitler came to the school, Jessie decided straight away that he was bad. She told me that she saw it in his eyes, a kind of 'enemyness', as though he had been sent to be on Master Hanley's side. The very first day, when Master Hanley started about the map and the bits that were red and how Germany was going to take over the world, he put up his hand.

'What is it boy?' Master Hanley was annoyed. 'I don't like to be interrupted.'

'Sorry *a mháistir*. Only I met Mr Hitler myself,' he said. I remember the way we all gasped. To tell the truth, we could hardly believe it. None of us had ever met anybody. It was even a kind of miracle that we had somebody in our class that had met a famous man.

'Did you begod?' Master Hanley said. He was suspicious. 'Where was that at all?'

'In Berlin. I was only very small. Only about two. It was before the war. He shook me by the hand.'

'Did he begod?'

'He did *a mháistir*. And he said something to me but I can't remember what it was.'

The boy held out his right hand as if we might be able to see the mark of Hitler's fingers on it, and Master Hanley looked down at it. He studied it for a moment and then he looked up. 'What is it you said your father was, boy?'

'Well, he has an even more important job now, but he was a reporter in a newspaper then *a mháistir*. A Dublin newspaper.'

'I suppose that was why he was in Berlin?'

The boy said that it was.

'I suppose he wrote something about Mr Hitler?'

'He did,' the boy said. 'He said Mr Hitler was the greatest man that ever lived.' Master Hanley smiled.

'*An-mhaith,*' he said.

After that Jessie hated the boy who met Hitler, and I had no choice but to hate him too.

2

WE HEAR ABOUT THE INVASION

My mam and dad

My house is not a big one, but it is big enough for my mam, my dad and me. I have no brothers or sisters. I had a sister once but she died of scarlet fever when she was very small. That is so long ago that I do not even remember her face. My house has a small porch on the outside that is always full of the smell of geraniums because my mam has hundreds of geraniums. Maybe she has thousands. Inside there is one big kitchen with a table in the middle and a big range that my mam cooks on. The stairs goes up the side of the kitchen. There are two bedrooms upstairs. The big one belongs to my mam and dad. The little one is mine. We call it the box room, I suppose because it is about the size of a very large box. It suits me fine. It looks out on the sea and in the morning the first thing I do is look out to see what ships have come into the harbour.

Sometimes there is a little limping ship that has come in on its way from Venezuela or some other foreign port and has been bombed. The German aeroplanes and submarines are always watching the ships that pass Ireland. Sometimes they are ships that carry food or ammunition to England. The Germans attack these ships. Sometimes if they are very badly damaged the bombed ships come into the harbour because they are safe here. Ireland is not in the war because Mr de Valera, our Taoiseach, said that Ireland was too small a country to be attacking anybody.

When my dad reads stories out of the paper about the terrible bombings in England he always says, 'Thank God for de Valera for keeping us out of the war.' My dad always votes for de Valera and so does my mam. Sometimes he sings a song that goes, 'Vote vote vote for de Valera'. My mam laughs at him when he sings that, and says, 'Will you go away out of that with your de Valera!'

I remember the night that Dad came home late and said that there was big news. Mam said he should sit down first and have his tea, so he did, but I could see that he was very excited about something. The funny thing was that although we called it 'tea' there was really no tea at all. This was because everything was rationed. You had to have a special card and this card told the shopkeeper how much tea or sugar you could get. The shopkeepers would only give you that amount. There was a shortage of all kinds of food during the war. We never had enough in our house and that night we had no tea for the pot. Instead my mam warmed milk on the range and we had hot milk and bread fried in dripping, and Dad had two rashers. Dripping was what we called cold fat – when it melted down it gave a lovely meaty flavour to the bread.

He gulped his milk down fast and ate one rasher. He gave me the rind because I always loved the rinds.

'Do you know what, Peg?' he asked my mother. 'There's going to be a new thing next. Will I tell you what? They're saying that Ireland could be invaded and we'll have to have every able-bodied man ready to defend the country.'

My Mam's face went white all of a sudden. She made a small sound like a little pup yelping, and she put her hand down on Dad's. Her hand was small and soft and white. She had been a dress-maker and she had very long fingers, which is a great advantage for needlework. But my Dad's hand was a farmer's hand. It was strong and red from the open air and the sun. I remember that. Her small white hand on his strong red one.

'What is this about invasion, Mick?' she said. 'Sure who would invade Ireland?'

'Do you know, they say the Germans might invade us.' He ate the second rasher in two big bites. I was disappointed about that because I had my eye on it and I was hoping he wasn't too hungry. Sometimes he left the eye of the rasher for me but tonight he was too excited about his big news. He just swallowed it down in two bites. 'See, we're the back door to England. If the Germans could capture us, they could open a second front. England wouldn't be able to defend herself from two sides. If the Germans had planes over here they'd be able to bomb anywhere in England.'

'But the Germans have no interest in us.'

'It isn't only the Germans, Peg. The British might do it too. They're saying that the British might invade us first to stop the Germans taking over. We could have the two of them fighting over us. We'd have to be ready for anything.'

'Oh Mick,' my mam said. 'Don't you go joining anything. There's plenty younger men than you.'

My dad shook his head. 'The way it is, Peg, I have to do it. I was never one to keep my head down and you know it.'

So my dad was the second person to join the new army. The first was Mr Jack Waite, a farmer. The next one to join was Master Hanley. My dad said it was fine of Mr Jack Waite to join because he was a Protestant and he was always very fond of England and he wouldn't be too happy if it was England that invaded us and he had to fight the English. My Dad said it showed he was a true Irishman never mind what people said.

The next day in school Master Hanley was full of the new army. He spent half the morning talking about it and boasting about all the guns and bombs they were going to have. Our class were half-asleep by the end of it. 'It will be called the LDF,' says he. 'The Local Defence Force.'

He said the name as if it was one of the grand names of regiments that you would hear of, like the Munster Fusiliers, or the King's Own Scottish Borderers. I thought that LDF was a fairly poor name for a part of the army. 'We will defend ourselves against the threat from Churchill, of course. Did you know, boys and girls, that Churchill has threatened to invade Ireland all over again? As if once wasn't enough for them! Begod, we'd show him the second time round the same way we showed him the first!'

Jessie really got into trouble that day because she stood up and said that she heard that the LDF would have to fight Germany too, that de Valera had said it and that her dad had read it out of the paper to them. Master Hanley flew into a temper. He said that Germany was no threat to Ireland at all. He said that the Germans would never invade us because we were neutral and because they were hundreds of miles away on the other side of England. 'Look at the map!' he told us. 'Look at it! Do you see that England is between us and the Germans? Do you think the Germans are going to go all the way around England just to invade a small country like ours?' That was when Jessie went too far. She had her bold face on, a face that I knew well. Whenever she made up her mind to do something really bold she had that face, a mixture of stubbornness and bad temper and mischief.

'I think you're a liar,' she said. There was a terrible silence all of a sudden. People didn't even fiddle with their pencils. Our class are always fiddling with pencils and things.

Master Hanley stopped breathing for about a minute. His face got very very red and his eyes started to swell until they looked as if they were going to pop out of his head and roll around the floor in front of him. Then he let his breath out suddenly and whirled around for his stick. It was lying on his table and he fumbled it so that it fell on the floor. He ran around the back of the table and picked the stick up from the floor.

'*Tar anseo!*' he shouted. 'Come up you brazen hussy!'

Jessie didn't go up though.

Our classroom has long oak benches that eight or nine people sit on together and Jessie's place was in the middle of the last bench. Master Hanley walked down outside the benches and then he turned sideways and started to edge along towards her. All the other people leaned forward to keep out of his way. He had the stick in his right hand and he was slapping it hard into his left. He was talking too, but I cannot remember what the words were.

When he got near to her he swung out with the stick and it caught her across the elbow and she let out a scream of pain. But the blow started her. She slipped sideways away from him. He followed and kept swinging out with the stick. She slipped further away until she was out from the bench altogether. Then she ran to the front of the class, but that was a bad idea because the door was at the back. When he saw where she ran, Master Hanley let out a little grunt. He always grunted like that when he was satisfied with something.

'I have you now,' he said. He didn't say it loudly at all. He didn't even sound angry.

He cornered her under the map of the world. She turned her face towards the wall and her back to him after the first blows. He kept on hitting her. He hit her on the legs and the bottom and once or twice he hit her on the back or the shoulders. She sobbed and begged him to stop. But he was shouting at her and so I suppose he didn't hear her say she was sorry.

He was shouting, 'You dirty little trollop! You West Briton traitor!' and other things like that. We had heard him say these things before but he had never shouted them.

At last, when his arm got tired, he stopped and Jessie ran for the door. I noticed that she was limping and leaning a little to one side like the damaged ships that sometimes came into the harbour. When the door closed behind her

I looked at Master Hanley. There was a foam of white spit around his mouth and I could hear his breathing and it sounded like an old cow's. Then I noticed that the boy who met Hitler was crying. He had his head down on the bench and his two hands wrapped around his stomach like he had a pain in it. And he was sobbing and coughing as if he was the one that got the beating.

I thought he was a right baby.

3
—

I Bump into Master Hanley

My mam sent me up to Jessie's house with a present of a clutch of fresh eggs and a half of a soda bread. With the rationing, flour was hard to get at times and people really appreciated simple presents. I used to wear a soft cap sometimes in cold weather and my mam put the eggs into the cap and I carried it up in my hand. The half of soda bread was sticking out of my jacket pocket wrapped in brown paper. On the way up the brown paper got wet with steam and the smell drifted out of my pocket, and even though I was only after eating my breakfast my mouth started to water.

There was frost on the road and frost on the bare trees. When I got to the top of the hill I looked back down into the valley and one half of the world seemed to be a kind of dull winter green and the other half was white with frost where the sun hadn't reached into the valley yet. There was no wind and the bay was like a sheet of glass. It was so still that I could see the reflection of the trees on Corkbeg Island in it. I leaned over sideways and looked at it upside down and tried to imagine that the reflections were the real trees, and it was so clear I couldn't tell the difference.

I knocked on Jessie's door and Mrs O'Neill came out. I said my mam sent me up with a half of soda and a few eggs and to say that she hoped Jess was all right.

Mrs O'Neill said would I like to come in and see her. She was still in bed but she was getting much better. After the beating old Hanley gave her, the doctor called on Jessie. He gave her a note to say she couldn't go back to school for a while. Then he went down and had a word with old Hanley and gave out to him. We were delighted to think about the doctor giving out to the master. We all tried to make up stories about it, all of us pretending that we knew what went on. The truth is none of us saw it at all, but it must have been great. Old Hanley standing at the door of the school or on the doorstep of his house and good old Dr O'Sullivan wagging his finger at him the way he did if you didn't take your medicine and giving out yards to him. It would have been nice to see somebody giving out to a teacher!

Mrs O'Neill took the soda bread and the eggs and she thanked me about five times. She said my mother was too kind to be thinking of Jessica at a time like this. I was amazed by so much thanking and all I could think of to say was, 'Ah sure it's only a few old eggs.'

Jessie's room was bigger than mine and it had two pictures on the wall. One of them was a holy picture that showed Jesus and Joseph working together in a carpenter's shop. Joseph was strong and had a beard but Jesus looked pale and thin and I thought, from that picture, that he would never make a carpenter at all. My mam would have fed him up on pullets' eggs and soda bread and stew until he was a fine strapping young fellow like myself and able to take on those old Pharisees that we were always hearing about, and give them a good walloping too.

Jessie was sitting up and she laughed out loud when she saw me. She had light brown hair and that year she had it curled and when she laughed the curls all shook like tangles of straw around her face.

'Lad,' she said. 'I'm glad to see you!'

I didn't know what to say so I asked her how the leg was.

'Sure it's nearly better,' she said. 'But father says I probably won't be going back to school until after Christmas.'

'Bloody good!' I said. I had heard my dad saying 'bloody' often. For example, sometimes he had a drop of whiskey out of a bottle of Paddy and after the first sip he would say, 'Bloody good stuff.' Sometimes he said 'bleddy' instead, but that was only when there were women in the house. Not my mam of course. She didn't mind him saying 'bloody'.

I asked Jessie what book she was reading and she held it up for me. It was *Black Beauty*. I wasn't interested in horses so I didn't think much of it, but she said it was really good. She told me most of the story, as far as she had read.

'I got it from Sammy,' she said. 'His mother sent him up with it.'

Sammy was the boy who met Hitler.

'I thought you weren't going to talk to him,' I said.

'I'm not. I was asleep when he came and Mother got it for me.'

I thought about this for a bit. I was beginning to see that there might be some hope of getting to talk to this Sammy and maybe he might tell me all about Hitler. If Jessie could take a book from him now, maybe in a few days she would stop hating him and I might be able to talk to him. I had to admit, no matter what side he was on, he had a really interesting past. Most of the boys I knew had no past at all.

'He's living in the last cottage in the Middle Road,' she said. 'He came up by the Backway. Mother says he has a Dublin accent.'

'What's wrong with your leg anyway?'

'Do you want to see it?' she asked. She threw back the blankets and pulled up her nightdress so that I could see as far as her knee. There was one huge bruise from her ankle to her knee. It was purple in colour and had a blackish centre.

'That goes all the way up,' she said. Then she blushed. 'I can't straighten it at all and I can only bend it a little bit. I have to do exercises. The doctor says if I don't do exercises I might get a clot.'

'What's wrong with a clot?'

'The doctor says if I get a clot I'll have to get an amputation. That means he'll have to saw it off.'

'Bloody!'

'I'd have to get a wooden leg.'

I was very impressed. There was no one in the village with a wooden leg any more although there used to be an old sailor who lost his left foot in the Battle of Jutland. But he was dead and I didn't even know his name, only his nickname, which was 'Step-In-The-Dry-Patch'. I suppose he was called that because he didn't like putting his wooden leg into the puddles.

Perhaps wooden legs suffered from rot. He died when I was very small. If Jessie got a wooden leg she would be the talk of the parish.

'Wooden legs rot,' I told her. 'If you leave them get wet, they rot off.'

'I'd get a new one. Father would buy loads of them so we'd have a stock.' Jessie knew about things like that because her father owned a shop. She knew all about stock and float-money and profits. When we did simple-interest sums in school she was the first up with the answer. She could do simple interest in her head.

'I'd make you one,' I said. 'I have an old saw at home. I made a rifle out of wood the other day. It looks real. I'm going to paint it. I could make you a wooden leg out of an ashplant, that way it would have a bit of spring in it like a hurley. You'd be able to jump better than ever.'

Mrs O'Neill brought us up a glass of milk and a slice of the soda bread with honey on it. Mr O'Neill had beehives down at the back of their garden and he sold the honey in the shop. The beehives were like little perfect wooden houses and the buzzing was like the noise of a big happy family inside.

'Say thanks to young Michael,' Mrs O'Neill said. 'He brought you a present of the soda bread and half a dozen fresh eggs.'

Jessie said thanks but her mouth was full of

bread and honey and it sounded like, 'Planks Mitel.'

'Did Jessica tell you our good news, Michael?' Everybody called me Mike or Mikey, or Mickeen, but Mrs O'Neill never called anybody by their short name. She always called Jessie Jessica. 'Daniel and John Joe are coming home from the Navy next week. They have a few days leave and they're coming over. They won't be home this Christmas, you see.'

I said I was delighted. And I was too because Dan and J. J., as we called him, were great sport and they were full of stories about the war. J. J. was in a ship in the English Channel that was bombed and had to be towed home by another ship. He said his ship nearly sank before she got to port. He often told me all about the different kinds of ships – battleships and cruisers and destroyers and things. Dan was different. He was very excitable and full of ideas because he had a very inventive mind. He was going to be an engineer when the war was over. He had already applied to the naval college in Chatham in England. He had invented a special coat that had an inside and an outside and in between was filled with ping-pong balls. He said that if the ship sank the ping-pong balls would keep him afloat. J. J. said he was a fool.

'We're going to have a little tea-party for

them,' Mrs O'Neill said. 'Would you like to come?'

I was always up for a party.

'Maybe you might ask your mother and father to come too?'

I said I would.

She told me the day and the time to be there and I skipped all the way down the hill I was so excited. The hill is very steep at the bottom and I was skipping so fast that I wasn't able to stop. I found myself running hard and shoving my feet out in front of me like brakes. But they didn't slow me down. Instead I careered round the corner at the bottom at about ninety miles an hour and ran straight into Master Hanley. I hit him so hard that he was thrown backwards onto the ground and I certainly heard his head hitting the wall of Mrs Hawkins's house. It made a kind of hollow thump, like hitting a hollow tree with a big stick. I fell on top of him but I managed to roll off quickly. He was a bit stunned and he didn't start to curse at first. I was always a very quick thinker as a result of playing so many games, and I worked out in a flash that if I dodged around the corner he wouldn't see me. So I legged it for cover. I stopped when I got round and peeped out at him. He was beginning to sit up and he was using very bad language. He looked around to see who knocked him down but he didn't see me. When he stood up properly he looked everywhere. I would say he thought he had imagined me.

He didn't carry on to wherever he was going but turned around and went back up the village, rubbing the back of his head and cursing. I thought to myself that it was revenge for what he did to Jessie. It was a kind of ambush, the best kind because it wasn't planned. Nobody could call me a sneak.

4

Dad Goes Off to Training Camp

My dad went off with the LDF one Saturday morning. My mam was very upset and I heard her giving out to him down in the kitchen before I got up. She told him that he was to be very careful and not to get in the way of any firing. He was to wear his socks in bed because those army beds were sure to be damp. And he was to take his boots off every night and dry them by stuffing newspaper down into them because the newspaper would soak up all the wet.

He told her that it was only a training camp and he would only be gone until Monday, but she said that training was more dangerous because everybody was only learning. 'Suppose some eejit shoots off his gun by mistake? That's what happened to Michael Roche of Trabolgan,' she said. 'A soldier was cleaning his rifle and it went off and shot off his arm. Where would you be with only one arm?'

'For God's sake, Peg, I'll keep out of the way all right,' my dad said. 'Credit me with some sense anyway.'

It was a bitterly cold morning and when my Dad's company gathered out on the road their breath made ghostly clouds in the air. They all had bags of clothes of one kind or another. My dad had a proper army knapsack but some of the others only had sacks. They all had their green uniforms on and the long army great-coats. Their buttons were gleaming and their big boots were shiny with polish. An officer came on a horse and he had long boots that came up to his knee – shining brown boots. My mam said he was a lieutenant from the real army and had been staying with a relation out the country.

I saw Mr Jack Waite there with his back as straight as a telephone pole. He was talking to my dad about the price of conacre. My dad owned eleven acres of land, but he rented about another thirty from different people. That was called conacre. He rented seven acres from Mr Jack Waite. You could only rent conacre for nine months, which was something that always puzzled me. But my dad said it was for legal reasons and there was no understanding the law, and I suppose he was right because there were some very strange laws going around. Like the law that said you had to have a light on your bicycle. Nobody around here had any lights at all, but the road was wide enough and if you gave a shout as you went round a bend everyone would know you were coming.

The last to come was Master Hanley. I went around behind him to see if I could see the bump on his head. All my friends did the same because I was after telling them all the story of how I flattened him. My friend Jim Reidy swore he could see the bump and it was red and there was no hair growing on it. I couldn't make it out, but we all hoped old Hanley was going bald as a result of the fall. We were so sure Jim Reidy was right that we nicknamed him Baldy Hanley on the spot.

'Jessie's mother was down the other day,' Jim Reidy told me. 'I heard her.'

'Tell us! Tell us!'

'God she tore strips off him. She told him she'd have him up in court if he ever laid a finger on anyone again. Ever.'

'Bloody!' I said. I'd like to have seen Mrs O'Neill tearing strips off old Baldy Hanley.

The officer stood up in his stirrups and counted the men. The horse shied around and his shoes clattered on the stones of the road. Then he said 'Fall in' and all the men formed up in two lines. I was proud to see that my dad and Mr Jack Waite were the first two. Baldy Hanley was at the very back, the last in line.

Another soldier from the regular army stood just behind the officer and I could see by his stripes that he was a sergeant. The officer called to him – 'Company Sergeant Major Desmond.'

The sergeant stepped forward and he and the officer had a quiet talk. Then the sergeant stepped back again and shouted, 'By the left, march.' The whole group of men started to march off. They weren't very practised at it and a lot of them were out of step. I didn't laugh because I had been practising marching myself and I knew how hard it was to get the hang of it. Whenever Jim Reidy and myself tried it he would always fall out of step with me and we'd have to start all over again.

After a bit the sergeant got annoyed with the way the men were tripping over each other and falling around and he started to say, *'Clé, deas, clé, deas.'* That was 'left, right' in Irish. The men chatted as they walked and I could hear that what they were talking about was not very military. My dad and Mr Jack Waite had got on to the price of bullocks at Midleton fair. The two men behind them were talking about a hurling match. One man even started to do the funny new dance over from England that was called the Lambeth Walk, sticking his elbows out from his sides, twiddling his thumbs and wobbling his shoulders. The sergeant soon put a stop to that. They were all in good humour and laughed and cracked jokes at the gang of children following behind them. Only Baldy Hanley was different. He stopped every once in a while and made a face at us and told us to go back or we'd find out about it next week in school. Then he would have to run to catch up again. My friend Jim Reidy said that he hoped Hitler never invaded Ireland because we'd be lost altogether if we were depending on Baldy Hanley to lead the charge. He said, judging by the funny way he had of running, that he wouldn't even be able to run away without getting shot. He said Baldy Hanley should give up the army and take up dancing as a job because he'd be well able to do the Lambeth Walk but he couldn't march if his life depended on it. Jim was a very funny fellow.

We followed them as far as the Long Point. When they went round the bend in the road we waved and shouted 'Good luck!' The whole company, with one voice, shouted back to us, 'Good luck!'

When I got home my mam was after making porridge for me. I had been looking forward to that hot porridge all the way back. I could see she was upset and worried.

'Cheer up, Mam,' I said. 'Sure he'll be home on Monday!'

'For God's sake will I ever hear the end of Monday,' she snapped at me. She rushed out into the backyard and I heard her giving out to the hens. I didn't think I would ever understand grown-ups.

*

I was out trying to catch crabs off the pier with a bit of string and a piece of fat bacon when the boy who met Hitler came up to me.

'Was that your daddy at the front of the army?' he asked me. I said it was.

'Is he an officer?'

'No he's not,' I said. 'But I'd say they'll make him one before long.'

'My daddy was an officer,' he said.

I stared at him in shock. 'You told Baldy Hanley that your daddy was a reporter.'

The boy who met Hitler smiled at me. 'It's a state secret,' he said. 'He was really a G-man.'

Everyone knew that the G-men were the Irish secret service.

'That's all my eye,' I said. 'You're only codding me.'

'Cross my heart and hope to die,' he said. 'He

was only letting on to be a reporter. He was sent over to find out about Hitler. It was all a cover, that's what it was. I couldn't tell Baldy Hanley that because it's a state secret. That's why I said he was a reporter.'

I wasn't sure whether to believe him or not. The whole thing was too fantastic. Just then I felt a crab tugging on the bacon and I leaned over to look down into the clear, cold water. The piece of brown string went down into the depths, passing fronds of dark weed, jutting stones and tiny caves. Down at the bottom a large green crab was wrestling with the fat, thinking to himself that he was after getting the best dinner he had since the war started. The crabs around here hadn't seen much bacon since the government started the rationing. People didn't have anything to spare in those days.

I eased him up slowly, swinging the string out as far as possible because sometimes a crab would grab at a piece of weed and fall off, or even scuttle into one of the cracks in the pier. On the one hand you could think that crabs were really stupid because every time someone sank a bit of bacon they couldn't stop themselves from grabbing it, and as well as that they held on to the bacon even when it started to move and hardly ever got suspicious. But sometimes one of them would start eating the bacon fast and as soon as the string started to pull him up he would leg it for a crack in the pier. You could never understand crabs.

After a while I had him out of the water, four of his six legs clawing at the air. I swung him in and dropped him down at my feet.

The boy who met Hitler was staring slack-jawed at my catch.

'Yuch!' he said. He raised his right foot high and stamped down hard. I noticed that he was wearing black wellington boots. The crab made a cracking sound and gushed out in bits and pieces and a patch of jelly from each side of his boot. When he lifted his foot again the beautiful shell was in fragments and the legs were splay-ed out like broken branches.

'What did you do that for?' I demanded.

'I killed him for you,' he said. I could see by his face that he thought I would be delighted. I knew he was from Dublin and maybe city kids would not have seen crabs before, but still and all, to kill someone else's crab!

'That was my crab,' I shouted.

He took one look at my face and ran away.

'Good enough for you!' I roared after him. 'Bloody Dublin Jackeen! Why didn't you leave my crab alone!'

5
—
COME BACK TO ERIN

Me in my good jumper

My dad was full of stories about the training camp but none of them was really about war or fighting in any way. What I really wanted were some good stories about how to kill people with a bayonet or a bomb, or how to hold a rifle. He did tell me all right that the kind of hand grenades they were using had a seven-second delay, which explained a lot. But mostly his stories were about funny things that happened to himself or the others. Quite a lot of them seemed to have bad language in them because I was sent out of the room so he could tell my mam in peace.

So I was really looking forward to the tea-party in Jessie's house because J. J. and Dan would be there and they were sure to have something interesting to say about the war. I was particularly looking forward to hearing about submarines. I was dressed up in my good shirt and tie and a new jumper that my mam had knitted for me, and I had to polish my shoes twice before there was enough of a shine on them. Dad wore his best suit and Mam wore the dress that she wore to the Farmer's Union dance last year. We walked up in the late evening and the smoke from a hundred fires filled up the valley so that everything looked hazy and there was a sort of warm smell everywhere, even though the air was cold.

Mrs O'Neill let us in and brought us into the sitting room, where there was a blazing fire. Mr O'Neill was reading the paper and he got up and made Mam sit in his place. Then he put the paper down and rubbed his hands together.

'You'll have a drop, Mick?' he said. I never realised it before, but my dad and Jessie's dad seemed to know each other very well. This was a strange thing about adults. They seemed to know an awful lot of other people whereas I really only knew the people in my school.

Dad said he'd have a drop of Paddy Flaherty if it was in it, and my mam said she'd have a glass of port wine. My dad always called whiskey 'Paddy Flaherty'. Mr O'Neill poured out the drinks in the kitchen and brought them in. He had a glass of lemonade for me but I was more interested in tasting the wine. It was in a tiny delicate glass that was shaped like one of the tulips that Jessie and I stole from Mrs Hawkins's garden last summer. It was a deep red colour. I tried to get my mam to give me a taste of it but she kept fluttering her hand at me to keep away. She got very red in the face. Mr O'Neill said that he was just reading in the paper about a hold-up of a bank in Fermoy and wasn't it a terrible thing and the country nearly at war to have these fellows gallivanting around holding up banks.

Just then J. J. came in and shook hands with my dad and mam. 'Well, well, young Mike,' he said to me. 'Was it you beat up our Jessie?' I said it certainly was not and he winked at me. I whispered to him that I was after getting Baldy Hanley and he mightn't be so fast to take a stick to anyone again for a while. Then Jessie came in, followed by Dan, and she sat on the arm of my chair. She was wearing a red dress with a sort of a harp on the front of it. She was still limping a bit.

'Well so,' Mrs O'Neill said, 'Will we go in? The tea will only spoil.'

The talk at the tea table was very interesting. Dan knew all about the way things were going for Hitler. He said the Greek army had defeated the Italian army, which was good because the Italians were up for Hitler. He said the Greeks were trusty soldiers and Greece would never be conquered. He also said that the Germans had fitted merchant ships with guns, which was a dirty trick. These ships went around the ocean pretending they were all innocent and minding their own business. But if they met a ship that was from England they would take the disguise off their guns and open fire without a warning.

'I believe Charlie Chaplin is after making a comic film about him,' J. J. said. 'I believe it's very funny.'

'Small difference it will make to Mr Hitler,' my mam said. 'That man is a raving lunatic.'

'I want the boys to stay at home,' Mrs O'Neill said. 'Would you agree with me, Peg? I don't think they should go back at all.'

'Oh Mother!' Dan said. 'We will not stay at home.'

'That'd be desertion,' J. J. said. 'What would our mates say?'

'It's not your war. It's England's war,' Mrs O'Neill said. I could see that she was very close to tears. 'What are Irish boys doing fighting England's war?'

Dan stood up from the table. His face was very pale and his voice was very quiet. 'I know it's hard, Mother,' he said. 'It's true I joined up for work. There wasn't any work at all, you know,' he told my mam. 'Not a bit. But there's more to it now. If we don't stand up to Hitler we'll all be taken over. He wants to conquer the whole world. That's why I'm staying.'

Dan in his uniform

He sat down again and gulped nearly a whole cup of tea. He was very red in the face after standing up to his mam. Dan was always very polite to ladies.

J. J. said he was staying because he couldn't let down his shipmates. Then Mr O'Neill said it wasn't the right thing to be talking about at the tea table and would we all give over.

After tea, sitting in the warmth of the fire, Jess and myself talked about Baldy Hanley and the beating he gave her, while the grown-ups told stories. She made me tell her the story all over again of how I came down the hill and knocked him down. Then she laughed until I thought she would fall apart.

Then the singing started and I had to do my party piece, which was 'The Rising of the Moon'. J. J. sang something about a very modern major general that I couldn't understand at all. He said he heard it sung in Covent Garden, which was an opera house in London.

'Sure I sang in Covent Garden myself,' he said, grinning. 'But only in the toilet!' Everyone laughed at that except me because I couldn't see the joke. I often sang in the toilet.

When Dan's turn came he said he would sing a special song for his mother. I think he said that because he wanted to make up for fighting with her about the war. Dan had a beautiful singing voice. He got up and stood with his back to the fire. The song he sang is called 'Come back to Erin'. It is a sad song about a mother who calls her children back to Ireland. Whenever I hear that song it makes me feel lonesome.

> *Come back to Erin, mavourneen, mavour*
> *   neen,*
> Come back aroon, to the land of thy birth.

Before the song was over Mrs O'Neill burst into tears and ran out of the room. Dan and Mr O'Neill ran after her. I could see that Dan was shocked.

Jessie told me that she was very upset because there were a lot of ships getting sunk and Dan and J. J. were going back on Saturday. Every day she heard about the Germans attacking some new place or sinking some ship or other. She was afraid that she would never see them again.

'Poor mother,' J. J. said. 'At least she doesn't know how bad it is over the other side. They been bombing London nearly every night. They sank a Yankee battleship not so long ago. The USS *Reuben James* she was. West of Iceland. It appears Hitler is afraid of no one.'

'Yes, and look at the way he turned on Russia,' my dad said.

'They say he's nearly in Moscow now.'

My dad shook his head. 'It looks bad, J. J.'

'Don't tell Mum,' J. J. said. 'She thinks we're winning.'

Later, as we walked home, my dad said that J. J. and Dan were two good boys but he thought they should stay home. Then he named three people who used to be in England. One was a mechanic in the Air Force and the other two were soldiers. They had all deserted in the last month.

'Rats leaving a sinking ship,' my mother said.

My father looked at her strangely. 'I never thought I'd hear you say that, Peg,' he said. 'I thought you were all for everyone staying at home?'

My mam caught his arm and hugged him close. 'I worry, Mick. But I wouldn't be so fond of you if you were a coward. I can't stand people running away from things.'

They were after getting a bit ahead of me on the path and the moon was out so I could see them as clear as daylight. They were both tall, but my dad was a good head taller. He took his hand out of hers and wrapped it around her shoulder. They were tall and strong and beautiful. That was my mam and dad.

6
—

THE INSIDE STORY

Jessie came back to school after Christmas and I noticed that Baldy Hanley left her alone. Mrs O'Neill called to the school every day to collect her at first and I usually walked them home. Jessie still had a bit of a limp but it didn't stop her running when she wanted to. Mrs O'Neill said J. J. and Dan were fine and that she was getting postcards from them often.

That was the time that the Germans dropped bombs on Dublin and everyone was talking about it and about how many people were injured. The night it happened was 2 January. When we heard the news first everyone thought Germany was going to invade and all the LDF were called up. My dad was out on coast-watching duty for the whole week and he was so tired that he was falling asleep over his dinner. Every day we expected to hear gunfire from the coast and my mam didn't sleep at night but kept getting up to listen out of her bedroom window and to look out for the signal rockets.

Then as the days went on, everyone calmed down. It seemed the bombing was an accident or a warning to us to keep out of the war and the Germans weren't coming after all. The LDF were able to get back to their usual work and everyone breathed a sigh of relief. My dad said that they were all worried and they had been issued with ammunition and given their orders.

One day, coming home from school on my own, I heard shouting. It was coming from the other side of the ditch in Hartnett's bog. I climbed up on the branch of a beech tree and had a good look in. There were three big boys in there and they had Sammy, the boy who met Hitler, and they were calling him names. They were saying he was a spy and that he would send a signal to Hitler to show him where to drop bombs and they were saying awful things about his mam and dad. Sammy was crying out loud. I watched for a bit but I didn't want to be seen because they were big boys and they were a lot stronger than me. But when one of them kicked Sammy in the knee I got really annoyed, forgot that I was supposed to be hiding, and shouted out, 'That was a dirty rotten trick, Harry Kiely!'

Then the three of them turned on me and I

had to jump down and run as fast as my legs could carry me. I managed to get to our house before they caught me because I was used to running and they weren't. Harry Kiely was fat anyway. Once I got to the door I started to shout at them.

'Yah! Fatty Kiely with a fatty belly! You couldn't catch a fly!' When Fatty Kiely made a dive for me I ducked inside the door and shut it fast. When they started to go away I opened it again and shouted something else. This time they didn't even bother to turn around.

But I paid for it the next day because they kept bumping into me and knocking me down in the playground. Baldy Hanley was watching them too, but he didn't say a thing because he hates me anyway. Fatty kept calling me 'foxy' on account of my red hair but I didn't care because my mam says that it's not red at all, but red-gold, and that my freckles are a sign of good breeding. And I agree with her. I always say, 'Sticks and stones may break my bones but names will never hurt me.'

But that was how I made friends with Sammy, the boy who met Hitler. When you save someone's life you have to talk to them. He came up to me in the yard before the bell rang and said I was after saving his life from Fatty Kiely.

That day I made sure I wasn't walking home

with Jessie because she was sure to be furious if she found me talking to him. Instead I went home with Sammy. We had a very interesting conversation. He told me that Hitler was very small. I said that he was after creating a lot of trouble for someone as small as he was and it was usually big fat people who started all the trouble. He agreed with me because the two of us were thinking about Fatty Kiely, but he said that the whole problem was because Hitler had been at the same school as the King of England and they were always fighting. He said the King of England was a terrible bully and he always picked on Hitler for being small.

Sammy

Sammy also said that Hitler was famous in Germany for getting jobs for people. He said that if someone was out of work they would only have to ring up Hitler and he would fix them up.

'Did your dad really meet him?'

He nodded his head slowly. 'He gave him a medal.'

'A medal? What for?' I had heard about the Iron Cross.

'Oh,' he said, as if he couldn't care less, 'it was for saving his life.'

'Oh bloody!' I said. I really was amazed.

It seems that years ago when Sammy was only two and himself and his dad were in Berlin, Sammy's dad did Hitler a good turn. It seems that Hitler was after tripping on his way across the train tracks in Berlin. He was lying there with his foot stuck in something and the Berlin train was coming down the tracks. Sammy was able to make exactly the same sound that the train would make and he could make the whistle too. I was still only learning how to whistle but my dad said I was making a good go of it. He started off moving his elbows backwards and forwards slowly like the wheels on a train, then he let out a fearful shriek that sounded just like a whistle, then he started shunting and hissing and his elbows got faster. He was the closest thing to a train that I had ever seen in a human being before.

Anyway Sammy's dad happened to be passing at the time that Hitler tripped and he heard Hitler roaring for help. Of course his dad spoke perfect German and he knew at once that there was someone stuck in a train track so he rushed out in front of the train and waved and waved until the train stopped. It came to a stop only about six inches from Sammy's dad. That's when Hitler decided to give him the medal.

'Was it the Iron Cross?' I asked.

He shook his head. 'I forget,' he said. 'When my dad was shot they took all that away. It might have been iron but I think it wasn't. I think it was just metal.'

Just then I heard my mam calling across the gardens for me to come in for the tea and I had to go, but I made up my mind to find out more about it some other day because I never heard anything like it before. I was dying to tell my dad when I got home. That was just the kind of thing that he would be interested in.

I was already almost home when I stopped dead on the street and thought, 'He said his dad was shot!' I felt as if there was a big lump in my throat and I swallowed hard five times to get rid of it. Then I said 'Bloody!' quietly to myself because I was thinking that some people had all the luck. Here was a boy who met the most famous man in the world and on top of that his father was shot. Not that I wanted my dad shot, but it was just that so much adventure was too much for one boy. I didn't think I would ever have any adventures, and I didn't think, with my dad standing guard all night in the middle of no place and only rabbits to shoot at, that he would ever be able to save anyone's life at all.

When I told my mam and dad the story, Mam said I shouldn't believe everything I hear. Dad said the bit about Hitler getting stuck across the train tracks reminded him of something but he couldn't think what. Mam said that Sammy was a nice polite boy.

I was hopping mad. They weren't impressed at all. I was just after giving them the inside story on Adolf Hitler and they behaved as if I was telling them something about school. Dad hardly even looked up from the paper.

So I went out and told Jim Reidy instead. He was amazed alright. He said he had never heard of anybody that had so many adventures, outside of books anyway. He said the thing about Hitler getting stuck in the tracks reminded him of something.

'That's what my dad said too,' I told him.

'I know!' Jim said. 'I seen it in a picture. I can't remember the name of it but it was a cowboy picture. There was a cowboy that got

his feet caught in the tracks and another cowboy tried to get the leg out. Then the first fellow
heard a train coming. He could hear the noise
through the iron in the tracks. The second
fellow got on his horse and belted up the line
as far as he could go. He stopped the horse and
waved to the train and the train driver pulled
the whistle and shoved hard on the brakes.'

'Did he stop it?' I had only ever seen one
picture when my mam and dad took me to
Midleton fair.

'Begod he did,' Jim said. 'But it nearly killed
him.'

I said that the fellows in the picture must
have got the idea from Hitler, and Jim Reidy
said they probably did. But that night my dad
came up to the box room to say goodnight to
me and he said he was after remembering about
the train tracks. He told me the same story.
Himself and Jim Reidy must have been at the
same picture.

'I'd say they got the story from Hitler, Dad,'
I said, but he only laughed.

'Sure the film is ancient,' he said to me. 'It
was made long before Hitler.'

When he went out he took the candle with
him and the room settled comfortably into
darkness. I got out of bed and sat in the window. My window is quite deep and when I'm

sitting there I let the curtains fall back behind me. Then I'm in a tiny room of my own, a room inside a room, a box inside a box. I looked out on the moonlit bay and heard the seabirds calling to each other. I turned Sammy's story over in my mind and in the end I decided that the boy was a liar. I made up my mind that I would be up for Jessie and Churchill and against Hitler and Sammy and Baldy Hanley. I felt better then because I knew where I stood.

7

—

SNAP ARRIVES

Now it was Christmas, my favourite time of the year. The only trouble about Christmas is that it is a very long time coming. For months you don't think about it at all and then when the nights start to get long and the days start to get short and you have to come in early for the tea, you start to think, 'Christmas will be here soon.' From that day on the weeks are as slow as months. The minute Santy Claus comes into your mind everything starts to go slow, like a clock with dust in the works.

Christmas in our house was a wonderful time. On Christmas Eve my mam took out an old earthenware jug that was brown on the outside and shiny white on the inside. It was cracked all around the rim and the handle was gone. Then she got down the big Christmas candle from on top of the wardrobe and she put it standing in the jug with paper stuffed down all around it. My dad would have a big bundle of red-berry holly and we would decorate the jug with the holly. Then I would have to light the candle because I was the youngest in the house and my mam would say, 'May God bless us and keep us safe from this day on.'

Then we would all walk out into the dark street and sit up on the quay wall and watch the candles lighting up in every house in the village. Our village is a kind of half-moon shape along the side of the bay, and if you looked at it on Christmas Eve you would see a half-circle of little magic, twinkling lights.

The first Christmas ever that I remember, Santy brought me a wooden train and I thought it was huge. That was because I was only three then. I'm big now and the train looks quite small, but when the paint got chipped my dad painted it up with red paint and it still looks as good as new.

I usually woke up long before it was daylight and I would creep downstairs to see if Santy was after leaving any presents for me. I wouldn't wake my mam and dad at all because they'd only make me go back to bed. Then when I had my presents I would go up and crawl into their bed and light their lamp because they wouldn't let me have a lamp in my own room in case I knocked it over and started a fire. Dad would give out to me about waking them up but he wouldn't really mean it. I'd play with my presents in their warm bed and the two of them would snore their heads off until daylight. That was the way Christmas always started.

This Christmas Mam had invited Jessie and her mam and dad and Sammy's mother and Sammy to visit us after the dinner. She spent the whole morning fussing around and making buns and soda bread. My dad said that she was wasting her time making buns because they'd be all after their dinner and their bellies would be bursting with the food.

The first to come was Jessie and Mr and Mrs O'Neill at about five o'clock in the evening. I showed Jessie the books and wooden racing car and the little pup that Santy brought me. When I sneaked down the stairs in the dark that morning I got the fright of my life because when I was searching round the kitchen I stood on something wriggly and it bit me. I shouted so loud that Mam and Dad came down the stairs with the lamp. Then I saw that Santy was after bringing me a little mongrel pup with one black ear and one white ear and stubby crooked feet and I nearly died with happiness. I took him upstairs to bed with me and I kept him wrapped up in an old shawl.

Jessie and myself spent a long time trying to

think of a name for him. We thought of all the dogs we knew but none of their names really seemed to fit. He wasn't a Towser or a Spot or a Lassie or a Judy or a Jack.

When Sammy turned up he tried to think of names too but all he could think of were the names of Dublin dogs and they didn't suit at all. You couldn't call a country dog Albert or Tim or Growler. People would laugh.

Then Jessie told us that Santa Claus brought her a gramophone and several records. Her dad brought it down to play for us. She said she didn't wake up early at all but about dawn she heard a lovely song in her dreams and after a bit she woke up. Then she could still hear the song and it was coming from downstairs, so she ran down and there was a wind-up gramophone on the kitchen table and Santy must have been just gone because it was still partly wound up.

Sammy's mother was a tall thin woman. She was so thin that she looked more like a bundle of sticks tied up in a dress than a human being. Her face was pale because she always lived in a city and everyone knew that city people never got any good healthy fresh air the way we did. There were big brown rings under her eyes like someone that was forever crying, but her eyes were soft and brown and she often smiled a kind of small, kind smile.

We all sat down around our kitchen table and
Dad put slack on the fire and after a bit the
slack started to glow and the kitchen got as
cosy as the inside of an oven. Before long Mr
O'Neill had his jacket off and his sleeves rolled
up and Mam put her cardigan on the back of
her chair. We all had sandwiches – made with
what was left of the goose we had for dinner –
and then the buns were put out. In no time at
all everyone was complaining about being too
full and loosening their belts and waistcoat
buttons. My dad said he was as full as a tick
and everyone laughed at that. My mam made a
face at him and nodded her head to the plate.
There were no buns left on the table at all.

Jessie put on one record after another and
everyone listened or hummed along to the
tunes that they knew. They were all old songs.
There was 'Afton Water' and 'Alice Benbow' and
'The Harp That Once'. The records were thick
black 78s that had one song on each side. After
each song we had to wind it up and change the
side. Then a small silver handle put it into gear
and the music came out. The singers were Mr
Peter Dawson and Mr John McCormack and
their voices filled the kitchen and drifted out
into the clear night air. They rolled along the
street and out over the water and it seemed to
me as I listened that they drifted up into the

stars where they shivered on their lonely heights. Ever afterwards I couldn't look up at the stars without thinking that they were listening for the sound of Mr John McCormack or Mr Peter Dawson.

Then the teacups and the plates were cleared away and the grown-ups started to play cards. They were playing forty-five, which is a very serious game. Grown-ups get very serious over cards. I got down my old pack that was missing the three of hearts and Jessie and Sammy and I started to play Snap sitting on the ground in the sweltering heat of the fire. I noticed that Sammy didn't say anything about Hitler but once or twice he asked Jessie if her leg was all right. He seemed to be very worried about it.

'He shouldn't have hit you at all at all,' he said each time. 'It isn't fair to hit a girl.' And I thought about the time I saw Fatty Kiely at him and I wondered if Sammy thought it was all right to hit a boy.

It was while we were playing that Sammy came up with the perfect name for my new puppy.

'Call him Snap,' he said. It was such a brilliant idea that Jessie and I just looked at him with our mouths open. We felt like kicking ourselves that we didn't think of it. Jessie said that was the exact right name; I thought so too, but I didn't say so.

'Here Snap! Here Snappy!' I called. Snap was dozing in a half butter box that my dad cut down for him and he must have recognised his name straight away because he looked up and came over to me. I tickled him behind the ears and all the grown-ups laughed.

'Is that what you're going to call him, Mikeen,' Sammy's mother said. 'That's a comical name.'

My dad said that it was the right name, for he snapped at my ankles in the dark this morning. 'Which was no more than the rogue deserves after waking the house at four o'clock of a winter's morning,' he said. Everyone laughed at that too.

'Snap,' my mother said. 'Well I never heard of a dog called Snap.'

'He looks a bit like a Snap all right,' Mr O'Neill said. 'A bit of a snapper, anyway.' They all went back to their forty-five and we went back to our game but now that Snap was awake he was a torment to us. He seemed to like the taste of playing cards and before we could stop him he ate the nine of clubs. Every time someone said 'snap!' he jumped down on top of the cards as if they were a rat and if anyone put their hand down he would grab the sleeve and start to tear it apart. He ruined the sleeve of Jessie's cardigan. Then to crown it all he got so excited that he went to the toilet on top of the whole pack, and that, I may tell you, was the end of our game, for you can't play with wet cards.

Snap and friend outside our house

8

I Save Sammy's Life Again

One Saturday morning I was throwing skimmers at the water over by the sawmill pier. The sawmill wasn't working any more because there was no wood to be sawn down into planks, but the sheds were still there and so was the slipway that was used for loading the sawn planks on to boats. This slipway was the best place for throwing skimmers because you could get right down close to the water. I was good at throwing skimmers because I practised a lot. I could nearly always make eight skips and once I made seventeen, if you count very short hops. I worked out a whole theory about why it worked with some stones and not with others.

Anyway I was skimming stones and I had just made ten skips when I heard a shout from the water. I looked up and there was Sammy sitting in Jim Lacy's boat with the two oars out.

'I'm rowering,' he shouted.

'I can hear you,' I shouted back.

'Do you want to come out?'

'That's Jim Lacy's boat. He'll murder you if he sees you.'

Sammy shook his head. 'He said I could if I wanted.'

'Fair enough so,' I shouted back. 'Pull over here and I'll jump in.'

Sammy started to row but he wasn't very well able to manage it. He kept splashing and pulling the blade of the oar out of the water and twice he tumbled backwards into the boat. In the end, though he managed to get the boat over to me. I jumped in off the slip and gave the boat a bit of a shove off so that we drifted back out.

'Move over,' I said. 'I'll row.'

'Ah no,' he wailed. 'I'm able to row.'

'You are in your barney,' I said. 'I never saw the like of it. You can't row at all.'

'Well all right,' he admitted. 'But I want to learn.'

'Fair enough,' I said. 'I'll teach you.'

I sat down on the bench beside him and took one of the oars. I showed him how to keep the blade upright and how to lean forward, dip the oar and then pull back. He practised a bit and then I pulled with him and after a while we were able to keep going fairly straight.

We were out in the middle of the bay when I

heard Jim Lacy shouting. He was a bit far away to hear what he was saying but I could see from the way he was jumping up and down and shaking his fist that he was mad at us. We pulled a bit harder and soon we could hardly hear him at all. In the end he stopped and I saw him turn around and walk down to my house.

I said to Sammy, 'I'm in trouble now.'

'I suppose so,' he said.

'You didn't ask him at all, did you?' He just shook his head. 'You just stole the boat.'

'I only borrowed it.'

I rested on my oar and looked back at the wake she was making. 'You're always telling lies to people,' I said. 'You can't believe a word that comes out of your mouth.'

He said nothing.

'I bet your dad wasn't a spy at all. I bet you never met Hitler.'

'I see a mullet,' he said. It was one of those very calm clear days when the mullet come in with the tide and you can see them swimming by. I didn't even bother to look because I had seen hundreds and hundreds of them. Maybe thousands.

'What is your dad, anyway?' I asked.

Sammy was leaning over the side of the boat looking down for another mullet so I'm not sure I heard what he said, but I think he said, 'A bad man.' I thought he was going to spin me another story about his dad being a bank robber or murderer or something else really bad, so I waited to hear the rest of it. I was ready to laugh at whatever it was, but he didn't say a word more.

The next thing he was standing up in the boat and his oar was floating away. 'Hi!' I shouted. 'Sit down in the boat!' People often capsize boats if they stand up in them. Out of the corner of my eye I saw Jim Lacy and my mam and Mrs O'Neill standing on the Sawmill pier. Jim Lacy was calling again. Snap was there too; I could hear his yapping.

Then the boat started to rock and Sammy was shouting, 'I hate everybody! I hate you and I hate Jessie and I hate my father and my mother!' He stepped up on the seat and shouted the whole thing even louder and I tried to drag him down, but he twisted out of my hold and fell over the side.

I suppose he fell so far out because he started from on top of the seat. I leaned over to catch a hold of his hand but I couldn't reach him. Then I started to row with the one oar but the boat only crabbed around in a circle. Sammy went right down to the bottom when he fell in, then he came up again spluttering and went down a second time. I shouted, 'Swim for your life!' but when he came up he started to wail about not being able to swim. He was splashing like mad, wailing and spluttering, and the next thing he went down again.

That was when I decided that he was going to drown and I wasn't going to be able to row the boat over to him. I took off my shoes and my jumper and I threw the oar in on his side. Then I jumped in myself and when he came up the next time I grabbed him by the hair. Straight away he grabbed me around the neck and I started to go down too. Luckily enough I managed to grab a hold of the oar and hold on. We came up again and I saw water coming out of his mouth instead of shouts. I got a good grip of the oar and I started to kick hard with my feet.

After a few kicks I was up against the side of the boat. But now I remembered that it was very hard to get into a boat from the water and if I let Sammy go to climb in myself he'd go down like a stone. I let go the oar and got a grip on the side of the boat and I held on as hard as I could. Sammy's face was right close to mine and I started to talk to him.

'Hold on to the boat, Sammy,' I kept saying. 'Let go my neck and hold on to the boat.'

He was all right, I could see that. Only he was frightened. I kept telling him to hold on to the boat and after a while he took one hand off my neck and grabbed the rowlock. Then he took the second one off and I was able to swim away from him a bit. His teeth were chattering and when I moved he started to cry.

'I'll ddddd-drown,' he shouted. 'Ddddd-don't ggg-go.'

I swam around to the other side of the boat and grabbed it. With all my strength I swung my left leg up and managed to hook it over the top. Then I hauled myself up and fell in on top of the seat.

Sammy was still holding on. I took a piece of rope that was meant for the big lump of stone that Jim Lacy used for an anchor, and I made a bowline out of it. A bowline is a special knot that won't slip. J. J. showed me how to make it when I was small. Then I took Sammy's hands off one by one and slipped the bowline down over his shoulders. Then I got a good grip on it and started to pull him up. When he was about half-way in I had to tell him to hook his leg up.

He was lying in the bottom of the boat vomiting water for about half a minute. After a that he got better and sat up. The two of us just sat there saying nothing, watching another boat coming out for us. Jim Lacy and my mam were in it. I can't remember now whose boat it was, but Mam kept putting her hands over her eyes to keep the sun out and staring at me. I suppose she was thinking that I was nearly drowned. I suppose she was thinking that she nearly had to put 'Lost at sea' on my headstone. Then I realised how cold the water was and my teeth started to chatter too.

*

My mam didn't give out to me about the boat at all. Instead, the minute I got ashore she started to hug me and ask me was I all right. She said I gave her a terrible fright and I was very brave to help Sammy. And then in the next breath she said I was foolish and we both could have been drowned. All the time Snap was rushing around us and barking his head off. When she got me home she boiled water on the range and I had to have a bath in the tub straight away. I hate baths. While I was scrubbing myself and trying to make my teeth stop chattering I asked my mam about Sammy's dad. She gave me that grown-up look and said that I wouldn't understand but I should be nice to Sammy. I said I was killed from being nice to him.

'He has his own share of troubles the poor boy,' Mam said. 'We don't know how lucky we are.'

9

WE SEE AN AEROPLANE FIGHT

One day, Jessie and Jim Reidy and Snap and myself went rambling on the Commons. It wasn't really rambling because we had a job to do. We had to bring sandwiches and a bottle of tea up to my dad where he was on coast-watch over White Bay. The Commons was a big open piece of land that belonged to nobody. Before the war anybody could put their cattle and sheep on to it, but since the war started the army had taken it over. It was a great place for a ramble and if you were lucky you might start a hare or see a pheasant. It was a warm day in May and we could see that summer was coming. Snap thought that every hole in the ground was a rabbit-hole and we had to keep going back and pulling him away or he would have dug up half the Commons. I suppose he was too young to know any better.

Mrs O'Neill told Jessie all about the boat trip and I had to tell her the whole story again, but I said nothing about what Sammy said about hating people, because to tell the truth I didn't understand it and I wanted to think it over. Jim was full of talk about Baldy Hanley. He said that he overheard Baldy talking to an inspector in the schoolyard. Jim was very mysterious about it and refused to tell us what he heard at first. We begged him but he said he'd never tell us. That was only to make us more curious. We chased him over half the Commons and in the end we cornered him under a thorn tree. Jessie picked up a stone and I threatened to push him into the thorns and set Snap on him if he didn't tell us. It was all just a laugh and he told us easy enough.

'I heard Baldy saying something about that old stick he has and I knew from the way he said it that he wasn't too happy. The other fellow, the inspector, he says, "You went too far, John." He said it twice. He said that the O'Neills were after writing a letter.'

Jessie almost jumped out of her skin. 'O'Neills?' she squawked. 'About me?'

'It was over him beating you black and blue.'

'Oh God Almighty!' Jessie wailed. 'He'll murder me altogether now!'

'He will not,' I said. 'He'll be afraid of his life to go near you.'

But Jessie kept saying that Baldy Hanley would murder her and I could see that she was really upset, so I folded my arms the way my dad does and I said, 'Don't you worry, Jessie O'Neill. Jim and me will guard you.' She cheered up then and by the time we reached the place where my dad was on guard she was happy.

My dad's job was to keep watch on the harbour in case there was an invasion or in case any German or British submarines tried to sneak in. His station was on the cliff high above the harbour, where he had a good view of the sea. It was a very important job because Cork Harbour is one of the biggest in the world and my dad was stationed at exactly the place any ship would have to pass. He was really Ireland's first line of defence. If there was an invasion he'd be the first person to know about it. It would all be up to him.

He had a pair of binoculars and he was happy to let us all have a go. Jim Lacy should have been there too, but Dad said he was gone to see about his snares. Jim was a great hunter and often gave us a present of a pair of rabbits for the dinner.

We sat down on the grass while Dad ate his sandwiches. Snap went to sleep in the sun and we spent our time looking down at the harbour and trying to guess where the fish were. Then Jim Reidy shouted and pointed at the sea. I expected to see an invasion fleet, maybe a hundred ships, coming at us. But all I saw were some white lines in the sky. Dad got up, though, and studied them through the binoculars. Then he said that it was an aeroplane fight very far out, and he passed me the binoculars. He took out a notebook and wrote down the date and the time and that he saw aeroplanes fighting out at sea. He called the notebook his 'log'.

When I found the white lines in the binoculars everything looked clearer. It was almost as if I was out on the sea myself, looking up at them. There were about eight or nine aeroplanes chasing each other around and around. The white lines were like steam coming from their engines. They were too far away to see whose planes they were but I was sure they were English and German. I had to pass the binoculars around and by the time they came back to me the fight was almost over. We were very excited and whenever something un-usual happened we cheered.

Then while I was watching I saw the white line from one plane turn brown and then black. Then I saw flames at the front of the plane. I saw a man jump out but his parachute never opened. He fell down and down and down but he was too far away for me to see him land in the sea. I told the others what I could see and they all stopped talking, and when I put down the binoculars my dad was watching me very carefully and there were tears in his eyes. He turned away when I looked at him and said something about Jim Lacy coming back and sure enough we soon heard the cheerful shout and saw Jim come over the hill with two rabbits and a hare in his hands.

Jessie said nothing all the way home. I didn't know whether she was worried about Baldy Hanley murdering her or sad about the pilot that jumped out of his plane. When I asked my mam about it afterwards she said that Jessie must be very worried about her brothers. I couldn't see the connection. Her brothers were in ships not in aeroplanes. My mam said I was too young to understand, which is what an adult says when they don't feel like explaining something. That kind of thing is very annoying.

I think Jessie was right about Baldy Hanley murdering her, because next day in school he asked her every question he could think of. He gave her extra writing for not getting her sums right. He sent her out for coal for the fire, a dirty job that was usually kept for people who never did their homework at all, and then he kept her in from the yard because she got coal on her Irish copy. He was surely picking on her.

That rat Sammy sided with Baldy Hanley all the time. First he was our friend and then he was on the other side. I couldn't forgive him for doing it after him coming to my house at Christmas. I was beginning to regret saving him from Fatty Kiely. In fact I was wondering if I told Fatty Kiely something would he murder Sammy for me. I would have to make up something. The trouble was I was keeping away from Fatty myself since the time I called him names. I decided I would have to fight my own battles and I managed to give Sammy a good dig in the ribs when we were waiting in the *líne* to go in. He started to cry but Jim Reidy told him not to be a cry-baby and shut up, so he did. But Jessie was watching me and she made a face at me and I couldn't understand it. Could she not see that Sammy was on Hanley's side? Or did she know something that I didn't know? Whatever it was, it was a strange look and it made me think about a thing Jim Reidy's father was always saying, that women were a complete mystery. Then I remembered the book Jessie was reading, the one about horses – *Black Beauty* I think it was called. I remembered that Sammy gave her that book and I started to think that they might be friends behind my back.

Baldy Hanley started in on history the minute we were sitting down. There was a great battle going on in the Atlantic, he said. German submarines were sinking British ships every day. Thousands of sailors were dying. 'Even at this moment British and Irish sailors will be drowning in the cold seas of the North Atlantic. Imagine that. At this very moment.'

This was all meant for Jessie, and I watched her like a hawk because if she went for Baldy again the way she did last time, he would really kill her. But she sat up straight, very dignified, and kept looking ahead. She was so calm about it that Baldy started to make up worse and worse things. He told us all about the terrible way to die that drowning was, the choking, the cold, the darkness, the sharks eating you. In fact he was so interesting that Jess relaxed and started to enjoy it. Then when he saw that he wasn't getting anywhere he gave up and we had to do reading.

I watched Sammy too and what really annoyed me was that he kept looking from me to Jess and back again. Was he spying on us? I thought he had a cheek.

After school I told Jess that I thought she was cool out not to mind Baldy, and she said that he was *beneath contempt*. That was a new one. She said it meant that she hated him so much that she didn't hate him any more, and I said that I still didn't know what it meant. She said she was pretending that Baldy Hanley wasn't there at all and it was working very well.

'I think I'll try that myself,' I said. And I might try pretending Sammy doesn't exist either, I thought to myself

'It wouldn't work for you at all,' she said. 'It only works for girls.'

10

THE TELEGRAM

When Jim Reidy found the dead airman floating in and out of the sawmill slip, we were all sure that it was the man I saw jump out of his burning aeroplane. We were all very sad, especially Jessie, because it made her think of her own brothers. Dr O'Sullivan and Father Walsh came down and a lot of people stood around and watched. They hauled the airman out of the water and laid him out on the dry part of the slip. Father Walsh said there wasn't a mark on him and he must have died from drowning. He was German, judging by the grey colour of his uniform, and later they said his name was Friedrich Rau. He was buried in Corkbeg graveyard and a lot of people went to the funeral.

Around that time I had a falling out with Jessie. I don't know if it was something I said or something she said, or whether it was because of the dig in the ribs I gave Sammy, but she took up with him and I was left out of it completely. They used to go off playing together every day after school and Sammy had his tea in her house. I was miserable but I was too proud to let her see it. One morning I saw them walking to school together and I got mad about it. I hurried past them and as I passed I said, 'Sammy, tell her about the way your dad got a medal for saving Hitler.' I didn't stop to see how he took it but I'd say it gave him a nasty shock.

They wouldn't talk to me at *sos* in the yard that day and I had to play with Jim Reidy instead. All Jim wanted to play was glassey-alleys, which was our name for marbles. We had a very complicated kind of game. First we had all different kinds of marbles. The biggest clear glass one was called a pulker. That was the best one of all. A pulker was worth four ordinary alleys or two half-pulkers. If the pulker was blue we called it an American and if it was pure blue and not speckled it was worth an ordinary pulker and two alleys. We had a name for every kind of alley there was.

Then the way we played the game was complicated too. You had to flick the alley off your thumb. You couldn't throw it. When a game was starting, the person who owned the game, that was the boss of the game if you like, would call out, 'Lines clearance and banks!' I don't know why that was, but it was always the way alleys were played. Even my mam and dad played it the same way when they were small. Then everyone would step back and the fellow who owned the game would place his alley and then he would draw a line in the dust. He could draw the line as far away as he liked. Then if some-one wanted to play he would have to say, 'Lines to the line and at you!' Then he would step up to the line and shoot his alley. If he hit it he kept the other fellow's alley. But an ordinary alley had to hit a pulker four times. Jim had four pulkers and they were all champions.

You had to be in the mood to play glassey-alleys and I wasn't really in the mood. I played anyway though and lost three before the bell went. I was feeling very fed up about Jessie and Sammy and when I saw them going in the door together I felt worse and worse.

So I decided to mitch off from school. Baldy Hanley was gone in already, so I waited at the end of the *líne* and when Jim went in ahead of me I ran for the gate as fast as my legs could carry me.

I got outside safely and ran straight across the road and climbed through the beech trees into Hartnett's bog. I listened carefully but I couldn't hear a thing. I waited for a long time but nobody came out looking for me. Then I looked around me and wondered what I would do. I couldn't go home because my mam would want to know why I wasn't in school. I couldn't go fishing for crabs because I would be seen. I couldn't go for a ramble across the fields because I was sure to bump into Jim Lacy out lifting his snares, or some other neighbour. In the end I decided to go up to the top of the hill, where I would be out of the way, and see if I could find any birds' nests in the trees.

I sneaked through the beech trees further up. Then I crossed the road and went up the Backway. This brought me up past Sammy's house. I saw his mother hanging out a blanket to dry. I got across the road without her seeing me and carried on up through the gardens. I was very good at that kind of thing on account of spending hours playing cowboys with Jess. I think I would have made a great spy in the war because I could sneak in and out of very hard places and get away as well.

In the end I had to pass through Jessie's own garden. I could hear noise in her house and I crept in close to see what was happening. The postman was standing in the kitchen with his grey bag over his shoulder. Mr O'Neill was standing by the range. They were both staring at Mrs O'Neill. She was talking at the top of her voice. She seemed to be very upset. I couldn't make out the words but I could see that she had a piece of paper in her hand. I knew the piece of paper was a telegram because I had seen telegrams before.

When Westy West from Corkbeg was killed at the start of the war his mother got a telegram from the King of England to say he was sorry that Westy got killed. Mr West said that the King of England didn't care tuppence about Westy but that he was sending out hundreds of these telegrams every day. I saw the telegram myself. It said that Westy was missing, believed killed. Later an officer wrote the Wests a letter to say that he was the captain of the ship that Westy was killed in. He said the ship struck a mine and Westy was killed in the explosion. He said that Westy died instantly and that he was a brave boy who never failed to do his duty.

So I knew that Mrs O'Neill was after getting a telegram and telegrams are always bad news. I wondered which of the boys it was. Was it J. J.? Or was it Dan in the *Hood*? But the *Hood* was the finest battleship in the world. She could never sink.

Then Mrs O'Neill sat down on a kitchen chair and Mr O'Neill put his hands over his face, and I ran away, down through the garden, down the Backway and into the beech trees. I don't know what I was running away from, but my heart beat as hard as if I had just been in a fight. I thought afterwards I was running away from Jessie, because when she would hear the news her heart would break. Her two brothers were the world to her.

I stayed in the beech trees until the bell went and people came out. I saw Jessie coming out with Sammy and Jim Reidy but she went her own way home. I felt I should follow her and try to warn her in some way of the disaster that was to come, but I could not make myself do it. In the end she walked round the bend and I had to make my own way home.

Baldy Hanley was there before me, sitting at the fire smoking a cigarette. My mam was sitting at the table. She stood up when I came in.

'Well?'

'Well what?' I said. She hit me a clatter across the face.

'Don't you well-what me my lad!' she said. 'Here's Master Hanley after walking down to see what was wrong with you that you didn't go back to school after the *sos*.' My face felt hot and stingy where she hit me.

I just shook my head. I felt tears burning my eyes and the tears were not for myself, not for the slap, or the trouble I would be in when I told the truth. The tears were for Jessie and her mother and father, and for the poor boys who were dying.

'Explain yourself.'

I shook my head again. My mam looked at Baldy Hanley and I could see a kind of smirk in his eyes, even though his face didn't change a bit. I knew he was thinking that I was crying because I was going to be killed by my mam. But he was wrong about that.

'I'll be going so, missus,' Baldy Hanley said. 'I'll leave him to you.'

He went out on his own and my mam stayed looking at me.

'Explain yourself, my lad,' Mam said again.

I said that I couldn't explain myself, that I had simply run away.

'Run away from what?'

I said I didn't know. I said that I was fighting with Jess.

'You'll have to learn to put up with fighting with people,' my mam said. 'People fight all the time. And then they make up. That's no excuse for mitching school. You should be ashamed of yourself. Fighting with Jessie, mind you!'

'Ah Mam, it's more than that.'

'What more? What more than that?'

'Mam, Jessie's mother is after getting a telegram and I'm sorry that I'm fighting with her.'

'What? A telegram?'

'I saw her. She had the telegram in her hand and she was crying.'

'Oh mother of God,' my mam said. 'The boys.'

She put on her coat straight away and told me to stay home until my dad got back. I was to tell him where she was gone. So I sat in the kitchen by the dying fire. My dad came in about six o'clock. I could hear him stamping the mud out of his boots outside the door. When he came into the kitchen he grinned at me and said, 'Well, Mickeen, you're all on your own!' And I burst into tears again.

11

NO MORE HATING PEOPLE

The story was that the *Hood* was one of the squadron of ships that was chasing the *Bismarck*. The *Bismarck* was a big German battle-cruiser. She was considered to be the most dangerous ship in the German Navy and the English had been trying to catch her for a long time. This time she was caught trying to sneak out into the Atlantic. One of the ships that were chasing her was the *Hood*. They caught up with her somewhere up off the top of Scotland and there was a fierce battle.

The *Hood* was hit by shells early on in the fight and one of the shells went straight into her ammunition store. She blew up and 1,400 men were killed. Only a few people survived. Later, the other ships caught the *Bismarck* and sank her, but that didn't bring Dan back to life. The *Hood* was supposed to be the finest battle-ship ever built but her armour wasn't thick enough for the *Bismarck*'s shells. They went straight through like you'd put your finger through a cobweb.

Mrs O'Neill was heartbroken. I saw her at Mass the following Sunday, when Dan was prayed for, and she was as pale as a frosty tree. Mr O'Neill was nearly as bad. They didn't cry when his name was read out but Jessie looked up at me. I was up in the gallery looking down. When I looked into her eyes I knew that she was like a hurt dog and that there was nothing I could ever do that would take away her hurt.

Baldy Hanley was furious the next day because he went out of the room to talk to the other teacher and when he came back somebody was after writing 'Bismarck Sunk' on the blackboard. We all saw Jim Reidy writing it but nobody would say. Baldy said he would give us all the stick until we told, but we still didn't say anything. He walked up and down the benches slapping his hands together and shouting. He was in a roaring temper. He called us wasters and lousers and dirty rotten lying scoundrels. Then he said we were all traitors. He called us other names too that I hadn't heard before and he even used bad language once or twice. He was so shocking that the teacher of third and fourth class stuck her head in the door to see if everything was all right. He nearly ate her head off.

In the end Sammy stood up and said he did it. We were all amazed at that. First of all, we knew he didn't do it, so why was he taking the blame for Jim Reidy? Second of all, he was the master's pet.

Baldy Hanley looked at him with his mouth open for a bit, then he pointed to a spot on the floor and said to Sammy to come up. Sammy came up and stood on the spot and Baldy Hanley took up the stick. He started to slap it against the side of his own trousers and it made a loud flat sound like the sound of a stick on wet sand.

'Why did you write that on the board, boy?' he said.

Sammy said he didn't know.

'You are not an imbecile, boy. Answer me. Give me a reason why.'

Sammy still said he didn't know.

'Hold out your hand so.'

He gave Sammy three on each hand.

'Does that refresh your memory, boy? Why did you do it?'

Sammy had his hands stuck in under his armpits and he was crying. He said he still didn't know.

'Hold out your hand so.'

But Sammy said he wouldn't and he shook his head four or five times very hard. Baldy

Hanley was so amazed that he took two steps back. Then Jessie stood up and said, 'Leave him alone, you coward!'

Sammy looked at her as if she was after saving his life. I'd say Sammy was one of those people who are always being saved by others. He was a bit helpless in a way, a kind of fellow that other fellows picked on.

'Only because you hate England,' Jessie said. 'And I don't care whether you hate England or not, but my brother was lost on the *Hood* and you never even said a word about it. I hate you.'

'Out of my school the two of you!' Baldy Hanley roared. 'Get out! Get out! And don't ever come back!'

The two of them rushed out of the room and we heard Sammy roaring his head off outside in the yard. Baldy Hanley went down and shut the door after them and on the way back he mustn't have been looking where he was going because he tripped. He shot out sideways and put out his hand to break his fall. He caught the map of the world and pulled it down on top of himself. He fell down into the corner and lay there for about two minutes, stretched out with the world on top of him. Then he got up and threw the map into the corner. He sat down at his desk and put his head in his hands. He looked up once and told us to do the homework we had for the morning, then he put his head back in his hands again. When it came to bell time he sent me out with the bell and I stood at the door and rang and rang until I thought I would ring the walls down.

*

I was telling my mam about it at teatime. Dad was out doing a night patrol. There was an invasion scare again. Everyone was saying it might happen this time. So many ships were being lost at sea that everyone said if England had an airfield in Ireland they would be able to stop the submarines. But Mr de Valera wouldn't give them an airfield and Mr Churchill was giving out about him on the radio. Now they were worried about Germany invading, not England. There were soldiers and LDF all along the coast by night and day.

When I told Mam about Baldy Hanley putting his head in his hands she told me this story.

'Master Hanley has his own sorrows, you know, Mike,' she said. 'I'll tell you why he hates the English, and small blame to him. Himself and his brother were out during the Troubles, the time we were fighting the Black and Tans. One night in 1921 they were stopping at a house over near Killeagh. Master Hanley wasn't able to sleep at all so he got up and went out for a walk because it was a fine warm summer's night about this time of the year. Didn't he see the Black and Tan lorries coming up the road to raid the house where he was staying. He tried to get back to the house to warn his brother but he was too late. By the time he got there the Tans already had the house surrounded. One of them saw him crossing a field and they all opened fire. He had to run for his life. He never saw his brother again alive or dead. He doesn't even know where they buried his body.'

'God, Mam, he has right enough to hate the English so.'

My mam shook her head.

'It's always hate, Mickeen,' she said. 'People are always hating one another. If we keep it up at this rate we'll all go to hell for hate.'

I knew she was right for wasn't it hatred that started the war, and hatred that had me fighting with Sammy and Jessie, and Sammy said he hated everyone except maybe Jessie, and wasn't it hatred that drove Baldy Hanley to beat Jessie in the first place. Everyone hated everyone else and no one had any pity. If more people had pity there wouldn't be so much fighting and dying.

I made up my mind that I would give up hating people. I decided I wouldn't hate the

Germans or the English and I wouldn't hate Sammy. I had a big problem about hating Baldy Hanley though. Every time I thought about him I could see him flaking the daylights out of someone. And then I thought, sure he's a miserable bloody man; he's not worth hating at all. I fell off to sleep like that, thinking about all the people I wasn't going to hate any more.

12

THE SPY

My dad was called up the very next night. The quartermaster came round to every house and gave orders that the whole company was to assemble outside on the road at six o'clock the next day. He wouldn't say what was happening but we all feared the worst. My mam stayed up all night ironing Dad's uniform and clothes and my dad stayed up to keep her company. I could hear their talk rumbling away downstairs all night, and the result was I couldn't sleep either. I did doze off once but I woke up with a fright to find Snap licking my face. His tongue felt like a piece of sandpaper and my face was all wet. I took him in under the blankets and the two of us tried to settle down again. Snap conked out quick enough but I didn't.

I got up about five o'clock and it was a sort of grey morning. There was every sign that it would rain before the day was out. When I came downstairs the two of them were asleep in their armchairs in front of the cinders of the fire. I tiptoed around for a bit, trying not to wake them, but I couldn't find anything to eat so I woke Mam. She made me porridge and before it was cooked Dad was awake. He said the smell woke him up. He was very pale and worried-looking and he kept giving my mam long looks. Then he went out into the yard with a basin of hot water and stripped off to his waist. I went out with my porridge to watch him shaving.

'Is it going to be trouble, Dad?'

He shook his head. 'Never mind that,' he said. 'Mickeen, I could be gone a while. I don't know how long they want us. So I want to give you your standing orders. Mind your mother for me. You're the man of the house now. Don't let your mother do all the work. You can help with the washing-up. And make sure there's a stack of kindling for the fire all the time.'

He went on like that for about ten minutes, in between taking skelps out of his face with the razor. I said I would do it all and he said I was a good boy. Then he put on his shirt and buttoned it up. He gave me the soapy water to throw out for him and I poured it slowly down the shore, watching the bubbles gathering and disappearing. When I came back in he was fully dressed in his uniform. I saw that he hadn't finished his bowl of porridge or the slice of bread and butter. His cup of tea was still half full.

As he went down the hall my mam was walking behind him giving him orders. 'Mind you don't sleep in the wet now. If that Jim Lacy goes off hunting you're not to go with him. Don't go getting into any trouble. Did you pack the socks I darned for you? What about the *geansaí* I knitted last month...?'

The whole company was waiting for him. There was a different officer there, on foot this time, and two more officers watched the whole thing from a motor car. They were just smoking cigarettes and watching.

Then the company fell in and marched off and this time they were all in step and there was no talking or joking. I knew that they were all thinking about their wives and sweethearts and wondering if the war was going to come to Ireland after all, and would they ever see their families again.

Snap and I followed them a little way in the grey dawn but my dad called out to me to go home and mind Mam and so I went home.

My mam was sitting in the kitchen crying and I just went and put my two hands around her shoulder the way I had seen Dad do, and the two of us were like that for a half-hour by the kitchen clock.

*

After breakfast I went up to see Jessie. There was no school for us because Baldy Hanley was gone away with the LDF. I was going to make up and tell her I didn't hate anyone any more. I thought she might just tell me to go away, that she wasn't talking to me any more. I was hoping she wouldn't because she was my best friend before Sammy came. So I practised all the way to her house and when I got there I knew exactly what I was going to say. But I never got to say a word of it because she was full of excitement about the invasion. She showed me a gas mask that J. J. had brought home from England last time he was coming and we both tried it on. When Jessie had it on she looked like some kind of horrible animal, and when I had it on I could hear my own breathing. It smelled funny too.

Then we started talking about the fight between Baldy Hanley and Sammy the day before. Jessie said that her parents didn't give out to her at all. In fact they said she was right to stand up to him. They were going to get her into Aghada school and she would never have to go back. I was really envious of her. I would have been delighted if my mam and dad took me out of Baldy's class and sent me somewhere else. The teacher in Aghada was meant to be a really nice fellow with a big store of funny stories.

Then we started to wonder why Sammy took the blame for what someone else did. I said Jim Reidy should have owned up, but Jess said that it wouldn't have made any difference at all. I agreed with her in the end because Jim was my friend and I knew he wasn't afraid to own up.

But why did Sammy do it? Jessie said it was because his dad was a hero and Sammy wanted to be like that too. He took the blame because he wanted to do something really brave.

We puzzled over that for a long time. In the end we decided to ask him. We walked down to his house and knocked at the door, but to our surprise a strange man came out to answer.

'What do yeez want?' he asked. He had such a strange accent that we didn't know, at first, what he was saying. Then I worked it out and I asked him if Sammy was at home.

'What do yeez want to know for?'

'We want to play with him,' I said. The strange man laughed and I could see that all his teeth were black. He had dark-brown eyes and a small moustache, almost as small as Hitler's, and I noticed that there was a smell of stale porter off his breath.

'Are you Sammy's father?' Jessie asked. The

man said that he was and what about it.

'Are you the spy?' Jessie asked. The man gaped at her. Then he threw back the door and stepped out to us. Behind his back I caught sight of Sammy peeping round the side of the bedroom door. His face was all swollen and red and his eyes had big dark pools round them.

'By Jeez I'll give you spy!' he shouted. He lifted his hand to swipe at us, but we were too quick for him. We dodged out into the road. He followed, shouting bad language, and so we ran away.

We didn't stop until we were in Jessie's garden, where we knew we were safe. By then I had worked out a few things. I knew now why Sammy was crying when Jessie was being beaten. It was because his own dad beat him. Although my mam gave me a slap once or twice, she never hit me hard and my dad never hit me at all. My mam always said that a woman's hand was softer. I don't know about that.

I also knew why Sammy made up all those stories about Hitler and his Daddy being a spy and a soldier and being shot. It was because he was ashamed. Suddenly I pitied Sammy and I wanted to be friends with him. I realised that what my mam said about there being nothing but hate in the world was right.

I passed Sammy on my way home. His face

wasn't as swollen as before although he had a cut near his lip. His eyes were dry too and there was a kind of hardness in them. I looked at his eyes and I understood what Jessie said the first time she saw him: that there was a kind of enemyness in his eyes. He was kicking a football against the gable wall of Mrs Hawkins's house. I went up to him and asked if I could play too but he turned his back on me and wouldn't play. When I asked him again he picked up the ball and walked off home. I suppose he was upset because I had found out that his father wasn't really a spy.

13

BALDY HANLEY'S TROUSERS

Nobody would talk about him before, but now that he was here, everyone said that Sammy's dad was a right bad sort. All through the week while my dad was away preparing for the invasion, Sammy's dad was drinking in Maclean's. Every night he started some trouble or other. He complained about the way they poured his drink. Or he argued about a game of cards. Once he even started a fight and the Civic Guards had to be called to break it up. They would have put him in the cell in the barracks only he was very badly knocked around by the other fellow and they decided he was after getting his punishment.

My dad came back on Tuesday morning, He had a cup of tea and a round of bread and butter and then he went straight to bed. He was worn out, my mam said. And his face had a sort of a grey colour that I had never seen before.

That was the first time that I ever thought my dad was getting old. I was surprised about that because before then I always thought he was the same age all the time. I suppose I was getting big.

He sat in the kitchen for a bit talking quietly to Mam and tickling Snap's ears, then he went to bed and snored his head off all day and there was no use hanging around hoping he'd wake up and tell me all about it. Mam tiptoed around the house and she wouldn't let me make any noise either, so I went off to see how Sammy was getting on.

It was the first time I called since Jessie asked about his father being a spy, and I was hoping that his father wouldn't be there, or maybe would have forgotten about me.

When I got close to the house I saw Sammy's mother sitting on a suitcase on the front step. I could hear roaring and shouting from inside the house so I hid in the bushes and watched. I was sure I was going to see a murder and I made up my mind to remember all the details so I could give them again in court later. In a way I was really looking forward to that because the only person I knew who was ever in court got there for being drunk and disorderly. No one I knew was ever murdered or even had to give evidence in a murder trial. It would make me famous all over the village.

Sammy's mother had her head down on her hands so I couldn't see her face, but after a while Sammy came out and he was carrying a suitcase too. He sat down beside her on the step and when she looked up at him I saw she had a black eye.

I was shocked because I had never seen a woman with a black eye. Sammy saw me looking at him from the bushes and he dropped the suitcase and came over to me. I remember that it was a small brown cardboard suitcase. I remember that because no one in my family had a case at all. When my mam had to go into the hospital once we had to borrow a suitcase from Mrs Hawkins.

When Sammy came over to me I signalled him to get under cover but he didn't bother. He just stood there looking in at me. We were a good way off from the cottage and his mother still had her head on her hands, so I decided it was safe to talk.

'Is he a murderer?' I asked. 'Is he going to kill you?'

Sammy shook his head. 'We're going back to Dublin.'

'But what about your Mam's black eye?'

Sammy shrugged. 'That's because she ran away from him. When my Daddy was away with the Irish army, that's when she ran. She made me come too but I'd rather stay with my Daddy.' I could see that he was struggling to hold back his tears. 'She took the clothes and things and we came down on the train.'

I wasn't surprised. If my dad hit my mam I don't know what I'd do. I know Mam would murder him. She wouldn't put up with that kind of stuff. Then I started to think that maybe this was a lie too. He was back to the old story again, about his dad being a hero. Anyone could see that he wasn't a hero at all but a right bad sort, going around giving his wife a black eye and roaring and shouting at the neighbours.

I said, 'Don't start that old codding again!' He just shrugged his shoulders. I could see he didn't care whether I believed him or not.

'How did he find you? Surely be to God he didn't search the whole country? How did he find out you were here?'

'I told you,' Sammy said. 'My dad is a spy.'

Sammy's dad didn't even look like a soldier, not to mind a spy. He was a big ugly man with turned eyes. His back wasn't even straight.

'Will you give up that old story,' I said. 'Your dad is not a spy and he never even met Hitler. That's all my eye.'

Sammy got annoyed. 'I knew you didn't believe me. That's how he found us. Because he is a spy for the army. He's a soldier.'

I knew soldiers didn't hit women. It was against their rules. Soldiers were strong and brave like my dad and J. J. and Dan, and marched bravely to war. They did their duty always. Soldiers had a code of honour.

'Your father couldn't be a soldier!' I hissed. 'Soldiers don't hurt ladies. No soldier would hit your mother unless it was a mistake.'

Sammy started to cry.

'You don't know the first thing about it,' he blubbered.

Just then Sammy's dad came out and closed the cottage door behind him. He turned to lock it and Sammy gave me a little wave and rubbed his sleeve across his eyes and went back to his suitcase. He picked it up and waited, standing beside his mother.

It was only then that I noticed that Sammy's father was in the uniform of an army officer. He had the beautiful green tunic, the leather Sam Browne belt, the riding pants and the gleaming brown boots that reached almost to his knee. When he had the door locked he put the key in his tunic pocket, took his officer's cap from under his arm and slapped it on to his head. There was a kind of violence even in that movement, the cap slapping down hard on his head. He turned around and looked down at his wife and child and then he marched off down the road without a word.

After a moment Sammy's mother got wearily to her feet and picked up her suitcase. 'Come on, Sammy, love,' she said. 'We have to go home again.'

Sometimes our harbour is called a 'port of refuge' and that is why the damaged ships come in. As I watched Sammy and his mam going off with their suitcases weighing them down, I thought to myself that they had no refuge. They were like wounded ships, listing to one side or the other. They were setting out on a long voyage without knowing whether it was safe to go or not.

*

Hitler never did invade Ireland and neither did Churchill. The war went on in other places and people came and went. It was such a big war that the whole world called it the Second World War – except Ireland. Here we just called it the Emergency. J. J. lived all through it. He spent most of the war on a ship that went back and forth to the Arctic Circle, taking guns and planes and bombs up to Russia to help them to fight. But Dan's body never came back. He was truly lost at sea. Jessie's family put his name on the family headstone and the date on which his ship sank. In the end, of course, Hitler was defeated and most of the Irish boys who helped to defeat him came home again. J. J. did not come back, though. He got a job in England working in the Post Office, which was funny because that was the job he ran away from in Ireland.

We never saw Sammy again, and we never found out if his dad was really a spy or just an officer, or whether he ever did meet Hitler. But when I told Jessie what I saw that last day before he went away, she knew immediately why he was always boasting. I always said it was because he was ashamed of his dad, but Jessie said that wasn't it at all.

'It was because he had nothing,' she said. 'He had nothing else he could give us, only stories.' The way Jessie saw it, all children like to give things. Small presents are important, like the eggs my mam sent her when she was sick. Sammy didn't have anything to give except his stories.

'But they were all just lies,' I said.

'But they were interesting lies,' Jessie said.

*

One really good thing did happen, though. It happened to Baldy Hanley. One day he was thrashing the living daylights out of my pal Jim Reidy for some devilment or other that I can't remember, and he was hitting him so hard that the braces holding his trousers up broke and his trousers fell down. He was so amazed that he stood looking down at them for about two minutes.

We laughed and laughed and laughed. Even Jim Reidy, who had been crying and wailing for five minutes, started to laugh. When Baldy Hanley saw Jim Reidy laughing up at him from the floor he pulled up his trousers and he walked out of the class.

He never came back. I suppose he would never be able to take the stick to us again after standing there in his drawers for two minutes together. When we heard he was gone for good we said, 'Good riddance to bad rubbish!'

The following week we had a new teacher. He was a nice man and full of great stories. Of course none of them was true, but at least he had something to give us. We weren't used to that. The first thing he did was throw out the old map of the world. It was all torn after the time it fell down on top of Baldy Hanley, and anyway the new teacher said that by the time the war was over we would need a completely new map. I rescued it after school and brought it home. My dad put a nail on the wall of my room and I hung it up there. When my dad would read about the latest battle I would run upstairs and find the place on the map, and any fool could see that the crooked black crosses were falling back and Hitler would very soon be cornered.

Another surprising thing was that Snap turned out to be a lady and she had three puppies the next spring. They all had one black ear and one white ear. I gave one to Jessie and one to Jim and Fatty Kiely's sister took the last one.

But the best of it all was that when Baldy Hanley left, Jessie came back. After that we were the best of friends again, and that is the way we have been ever since.